Songs That Honor America

William Decker

INFOMAX COMMON CORE READERS

Rosen Classroom™

New York

Published in 2013 by The Rosen Publishing Group, Inc.
29 East 21st Street, New York, NY 10010

Book Design: Michael Harmon

Photo Credits: Cover Jemal Countess/Staff/Wire Image/Getty Images; p. 4 Paul Hakimata Photography/Shutterstock.com; p. 5 AVAVA/Shutterstock.com; pp. 6, 8 Digital Vision./Thinkstock.com; p. 7 Raphael GAILLARDE/Contributor/Gamma-Rapho via Getty Images; p. 9 Evans/Stringer/Hulton Archive/Getty Images; p. 10 Craig Barhorst/Shutterstock.com; p. 11 zimmytws/Shutterstock.com; p. 12 Jupiterimages/Thinkstock.com; p. 13 (mountain) James Tibbott/Shutterstock.com; p. 13 (hills) Charles L Bolin/Shutterstock.com; p. 14 http://commons.wikimedia.org/wiki/File:Woody_Guthrie_NYWTS.jpg; p. 15 (coast) S. Borisov/Shutterstock.com; p. 15 (new york city) upthebanner/Shutterstock.com; p. 16 (redwoods) Jeffery M. Frank/Shutterstock.com; p. 16 (river) Pecold/Shutterstock.com; p. 17 MANDY GODBEHEAR/Shutterstock.com; p. 19 oliveromg/Shutterstock.com; p. 20 Christian Petersen/Staff/Getty Images Sport/Getty Images; p. 21 Lance King/Contributor/Getty Images Sport/Getty Images; p. 22 © iStockphoto.com/omgimages.

ISBN: 978-1-4488-9037-8
6-pack ISBN: 978-1-4488-9038-5

Manufactured in the United States of America

CPSIA Compliance Information: Batch #WS12RC: For further information contact Rosen Publishing, New York, New York at 1-800-237-9932.

Word Count: 417

Contents

Feeling Proud

The United States is a big country. A lot of things make it special. It has different kinds of land. America has different kinds of people, too.

Americans love the United States. They feel **proud** of their country. They think that America is a good place to live.

It's important to honor America. It shows that you love your country. One way to honor America is by singing **patriotic** songs.

There are many songs about America. Some songs honor our flag. Other songs honor our land.

The National Anthem

America's most important song is the **national** anthem.

An anthem is a song that stands for a group of people.

We sing the national anthem a lot.

The national anthem was written in 1814.

Francis Scott Key wrote this song. The national anthem honors our flag.

The song tells us to be proud of our flag. It's a symbol of our country. A symbol is something that stands for something else.

When we sing the national anthem, we say that America is free. Freedom means that nobody can tell you how to live. This makes America great.

We also sing that Americans are brave. This honors Americans who fought for our freedom. The national anthem helps us honor our past.

Honoring Our Land

America is a beautiful country. We have tall hills and lots of water. We have farms and cities, too. Sometimes we want to sing about them.

One song we sing is "This Land Is Your Land." Woody Guthrie wrote this song in 1940. It tells us about America.

This song tells us about different parts of our country. We sing about different states. We also sing about different kinds of land.

First, we sing about America's forests. Forests have really tall trees. Then we sing about our water. America has a lot of rivers and lakes.

This song says that America is my home. It says that America is your home, too. This means that Americans are **equal**. This is the best part about living in America.

This Land Is Your Land

Americans live in many different places.
Woodie Guthrie's song talks about some different places where Americans live.

city

forest

plains

mountain

river

ocean

People sing this song a lot. Sometimes we sing it at school. It's easy to learn the words.

Honoring Our Past

Singing patriotic songs helps us learn about America's past. Some songs were written a long time ago. They're still important today.

People feel happy when they sing songs about America. Sometimes we sing them at school. The songs sound nice when people sing together.

It's good to honor America by singing patriotic songs. There are many more songs about America. Do you know what they are?

Glossary

equal (EE-kwuhl) Things that are the same.

patriotic (pay-tree-AH-tihk) Having or showing love for your country.

proud (PROWD) Thinking that something is good.

national (NAA-shuh-nuhl) Having to do with the whole country.

Index